Alice in Wonderland
Puzzle and Gamebook

by
Edward Wakeling

An imprint of U.S. GAMES SYSTEMS, INC.
179 Ludlow Street
Stamford, CT 06902 USA

Library of Congress Catalog Card Number: 93-080602

ISBN 1-57281-006-8

Printed in USA

10 9 8 7 6 5 4 3 2

CONTENTS

Page

Introduction 5

The Puzzles and Games:

1. The Rabbit Hole 6
2. The Lovely Garden 7
3. Little Cakes (1) 8
4. Two Brothers and a Box 9
5. Who in the World Am I? 10
6. How Puzzling It All Is! 11
7. Who Goes Where? 12
8. Character Crossword (1) 13
9. Doublets 14
10. Three Squares 15
11. Word Jumble 16
12. Character Crossword (2) 17
13. Who's Telling the Truth? 18
14. The Thirty Letter Game 19
15. Thimbles 20
16. Character Wordsearch (1) 21
17. On the Roof! 22
18. Little Cakes (2) 23
19. A Stick I Found 24
20. A Mysterious Number 25
21. Cryptogram 26
22. Who's Coming to Dinner? 27
23. Upside Down 28
24. Dreaming 29
25. Consecutive Letters 30

26. Eggs in a Row 31
27. A Serpentile Letter 32
28. Postal Magic Square 33
29. A Number of Letters 34
30. Cipher 35
31. Fair Shares 38
32. Transformation 40
33. Cat Food 41
34. Which Clock? 42
35. The Hatter's Riddle 43
36. A Mad Tea Party 44
37. Painted Cubes 45
38. An Odd Card 46
39. Court Circular 47
40. Off With Their Heads! 50
41. Arithmetical Croquet 51
42. A Tale of More Heads 54
43. The King's First Problem 55
44. The Rule of Three 57
45. A Lesson in Squaring 59
46. A Lesson in Uglification 60
47. Character Wordsearch (2) 61
48. Diagonal Acrostic 62
49. The King's Second Problem 63
50. The Queen's Problem 64
51. Lanrick 65
52. A Russian's Sons 67
53. Making Words 68
54. Alice in Wonderland Acrostic 69

Solutions 71

Introduction

This *Alice in Wonderland Puzzle and Game Book* is written specifically to go with the playing cards that are used for the game "Alice in Wonderland." Although separate from the card game, they add a further level of interest and provide a wealth of other activities to challenge and entertain the reader. Lewis Carroll's book, *Alice's Adventures in Wonderland*, was first published in 1865. The pictorial playing cards were devised many years later, using John Tenniel's original illustrations for the book. These were specially coloured by Gertrude Thomson for the initial set of forty-eight playing cards. More recently, six extra cards have been designed and drawn by Brian Partridge. Over half of the puzzles in this book were invented by Lewis Carroll to entertain his many child friends. He intended writing a puzzle book and during his life he collected and invented a number of puzzles and riddles. He also invented some interesting games for groups to play. Some of these are also reproduced here. I have added some further puzzles so that the book fits the illustrations of each playing card. The puzzles should appeal to a wide age range. Some of the puzzles are very easy, but others will tax the sharpest brain. Answers will be found at the end of the book. I hope you enjoy trying these puzzles and games.

Edward Wakeling

Puzzle #1 / The Rabbit Hole

Suddenly a White Rabbit with pink eyes, dressed in a waistcoat, and with a pocket watch ran close by Alice. She ran after it and was just in time to see it pop down a large rabbit hole. In another moment down went Alice after it.

"TOO LATE," said the RABBIT.

Go through his burrow and find different words you can make using the letters you meet on the way down. For example, you can make DISH.

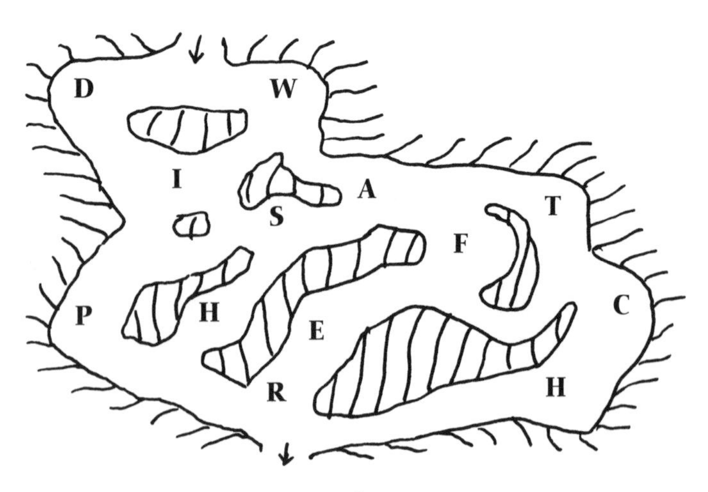

Puzzle #2 / The Lovely Garden

Behind a low curtain, Alice found a little door that led to the loveliest garden you ever saw. But she was too big to get through. On a glass table she found a little bottle marked "DRINK ME." She ventured to taste it and very soon finished it off.

ALICE AND THE BOTTLE.

Follow this maze and see if you can get into the garden.

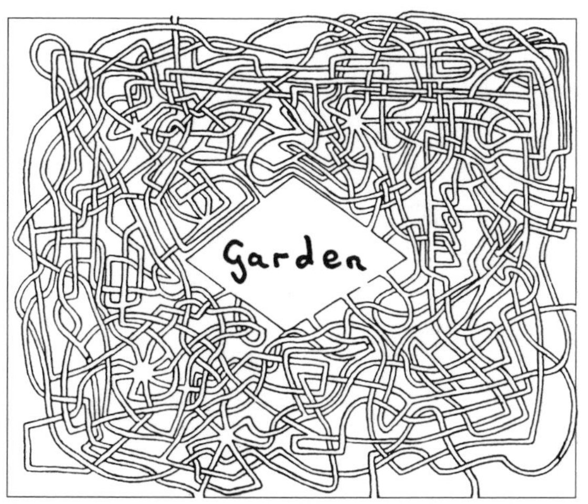

Puzzle #3 / Little Cakes (l)

THE BOTTLE.

"What a curious feeling!" said Alice. "I must be shutting up like a telescope." When she got to the door, she found she had forgotten the little golden key. Her eye fell on a little glass box that was lying under the table. In it was a small cake on which the words "EAT ME" were marked.

If Alice had nine cakes, she could arrange them in a pattern. She could put them into rows of three. Make eight rows of three with just nine little cakes.

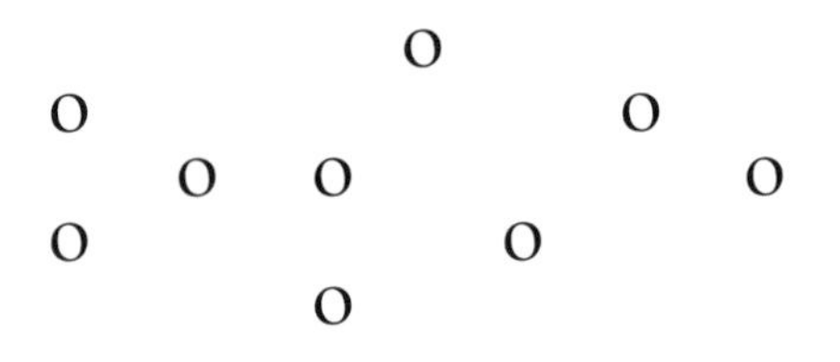

Puzzle #4 / Two Brothers and a Box

"Well, I'll eat it," said Alice, "and if it makes me larger, I can reach the key; and if it makes me smaller, I can creep under the door; so either way I'll get into the garden, and I don't care which happens!"

Here is a problem about a box and locks but no key. Can you find out what kind of box it is?

John gave his brother James a box:
About it there were many locks.

James woke and said it gave him pain;
So gave it back to John again.

The box was not with lid supplied,
Yet caused two lids to open wide:

And all these locks had never a key —
What kind of box, then, could it be?

Puzzle #5 / Who in the World Am I?

"Curiouser and curiouser!" cried Alice. "Who in the world am I? Ah, *that's* the great puzzle!" And she began thinking over all the children she knew that were of the same age as herself, to see if she could have been changed for any of them.

ALICE TELESCOPING.

If you replace these stars with the name of one of the children Alice was thinking about, you will make words. The same name, containing three letters, is all you need.

*** * * P T**
M * * * M
*** * * G E**
H E * * * C H E
R * * * R

Who was Alice thinking about?

Puzzle #6 / How Puzzling It All Is!

Alice kept fanning herself with the fan that the White Rabbit dropped. "Oh dear, how puzzling it all is!" she said. "I'll try if I know all the things I used to know. Let me see: four times five is twelve, and four times six is thirteen, and four times seven is — oh dear! I shall never get to twenty at that rate!

Here is the multiplication table that Alice recited:

$$4 \times 5 = 12$$
$$4 \times 6 = 13$$
$$4 \times 7 =$$

Why do you think Alice will never get to twenty at that rate?

Puzzle #7 / Who Goes Where?

The Rabbit ran away. Alice said, "Let's try Geography. London is the capital of Paris, and Paris is the capital of Rome, and Rome — no, *that's* all wrong, I'm certain. I must have been changed."

THE RABBIT RUNNING AWAY.

Some of the characters Alice meets are found in different places in Wonderland. Follow the lines that link each character to a place and discover where they are.

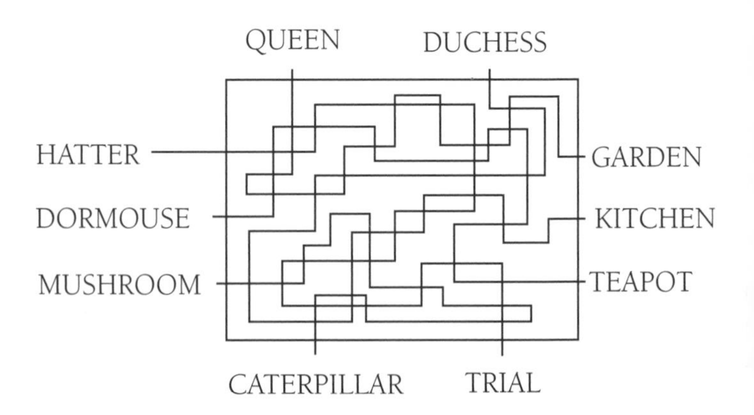

Puzzle #8 / Character Crossword (1)

Alice begins to cry as she fans herself. She doesn't realise that she is gradually shrinking again. Suddenly she falls into a pool of her own tears. "I wish I hadn't cried so much!" said Alice. She hears something splashing about in the pool. At first she thinks it is a walrus or a hippopotamus.

Complete this crossword to find some of the characters hiding in Wonderland:

Across:
1. In Hatter's riddle
4. Alice's pet
5. A gardener

Down:
2. In the pool of tears
3. To hide.

1	2		3	
4				
5				

Puzzle #9 / Doublets

Alice soon made it out to be a Mouse who was in the pool of tears with her. Alice told the mouse about her cat, Dinah, and a little dog. The Mouse quivered with fright and said, "Let us get to the shore, and then I'll tell you why it is I hate cats and dogs."

Can you turn CAT into DOG? The rule of this game, which Lewis Carroll called *Doublets*, is to change one letter at a time, leaving the others in the same position. Each change should be a real word. For example, this is how you change TEA into POT:

TEA
PEA
PET
POT

When you have changed CAT into DOG, try turning FOUR into FIVE.

Puzzle #10 / Three Squares

One of the wet and bedraggled animals that Alice met on the shore was a Duck. To help the animals get dry, the Mouse recited some dry history, "Stigand, the patriotic archbishop of Canterbury, found *it* advisable. . . ." "I know what *it* means," said the Duck: "it's generally a frog or a worm."

In this puzzle, draw these three interlocking squares. You must not go over a line twice, nor take your pencil off the page until all the squares are complete, nor cross a line you have already drawn. Perhaps you will be dry by the time you complete the puzzle.

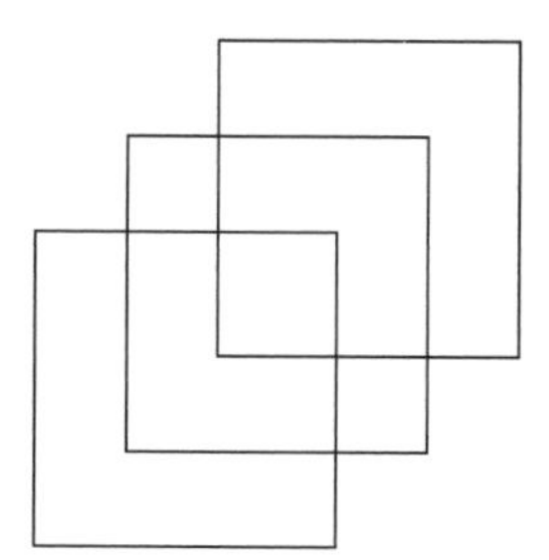

Puzzle #11 / Word Jumble

Alice also met a Lory. When the Mouse recited the driest piece of history the Lory said, "Ugh!" with a shiver. "I beg your pardon!" said the Mouse, frowning, but very politely: "Did you speak?" "Not I!" said the Lory hastily.

Here are some of the creatures that Alice meets on the shore, but the letters are jumbled up. Unscramble the letters and find out what they are:

LAGTEE
CUKD
ODDO
BARC
OMUSE
DRIB
PEGAMI
RANYCA

Puzzle #12 / Character Crossword (2)

The Dodo said, "I move that the meeting adjourn, for the immediate adoption of more energetic remedies . . . ." "Speak English!" said the Eaglet. "I don't know the meaning of half those long words, and, what's more, I don't believe you do either!" And the Eaglet bent down its head to hide a smile.

In this crossword puzzle, the clues down have been completed. Find two characters from Wonderland to complete the words across.

	A			E	
■	D	■	■	Y	■
	A			E	

Puzzle #13 / Who's Telling the Truth?

The Dodo suggested that they have a Caucus Race to help them get dry. Alice said "What is a Caucus Race?" "Why," said the Dodo, "the best way to explain it is to do it." All the creatures began running when they liked, and stopped when they liked, so it was not easy to know when the race was over.

Here is a puzzle about the Dodo and two other characters in Wonderland.

The Dodo says that the Lory tells lies.
The Lory says that the Eaglet tells lies.
The Eaglet says that both the Dodo and the Lory tell lies.

Who is telling the truth'?

Try to explain your answer.

Game #14 / The Thirty Letter Game

At the end of the Caucus Race the Dodo decided that everybody has won and all must have prizes. Alice supplied comfits for the animals. "But she must have a prize herself," said the Mouse. Alice found a thimble in her pocket, and the Dodo took it and presented it back to Alice as her prize.

Here is a game you can play with a friend, and the winner might even get a prize, if you can find a thimble. Write out the alphabet four or five times on strips of card. Cut out each letter. Put the vowels into one bag, the consonants into another. Shake them up. Draw nine vowels and twenty-one consonants. Make up a duplicate set for your opponent. With these you must make six real words (not proper names) so as to use all the letters. Sit where you cannot see one another's work, and make it a race. The first to use all thirty letters in six words wins.

Puzzle #15 / Thimbles

The Dodo said, "We beg your acceptance of this elegant thimble." Alice thought it was absurd to get her own thimble back as a prize, but she solemnly took it, bowed to the Dodo, and dared not laugh. Then the Mouse told Alice his history. It was a long and a sad tale.

In this puzzle, imagine there are two tumblers each containing the same amount of liquid. One contains brandy and the other contains water. Take a thimbleful of the brandy and transfer it without spilling into the second tumbler and stir well. Then take a thimbleful of the mixture and transfer it back without spilling to the first tumbler. At the end of both transactions, has more brandy been transferred from the first tumbler to the second, or more water from the second to the first?

Puzzle #16 / Character Wordsearch (1)

Alice offended the Mouse by finding a knot in its tale. "You insult me by talking such nonsense!" said the Mouse, and walked off. An old Crab said to her daughter, "Let this be a lesson to you never to lose your temper!"

In this wordsearch, see if you can find eight animals. They all took part in the Caucus Race.

M	M	I	T	D	E	C	F	M	P
G	A	C	L	O	R	Y	R	D	H
T	G	J	A	R	I	D	O	A	L
E	P	T	K	N	O	F	S	I	B
L	I	A	X	C	A	W	Y	M	E
G	E	Q	U	A	U	R	O	O	J
A	L	A	B	E	Z	D	Y	U	L
E	O	D	R	I	B	P	W	S	A
V	F	I	B	S	E	W	R	E	J

Puzzle #17 / On the Roof!

Alice found her way into the White Rabbit's house. She grew larger, after drinking from another little bottle, until she filled the room with one leg stuck up the chimney. The Rabbit tried unsuccessfully to get in. So he sent Bill the Lizard up a ladder and onto the roof where he dislodged a loose slate.

BILL THE LIZARD.

Then Bill inched his way down the chimney. Alice gave a sharp kick. There was a chorus of "There goes Bill!"

Using the same rules for *Doublets* as given in puzzle number 9 (page 14), change TILES into SLATE.

Also, go from KICK to LAND and from BOOTED to ROCKET.

Puzzle #18 / Little Cakes (2)

Alice put her hand out of the window and made a snatch in the air. The Rabbit fell into the cucumber frame. Next, Alice heard the Rabbit say, "A barrowful will do." A shower of little pebbles came rattling in at the window. The pebbles turned into little cakes.

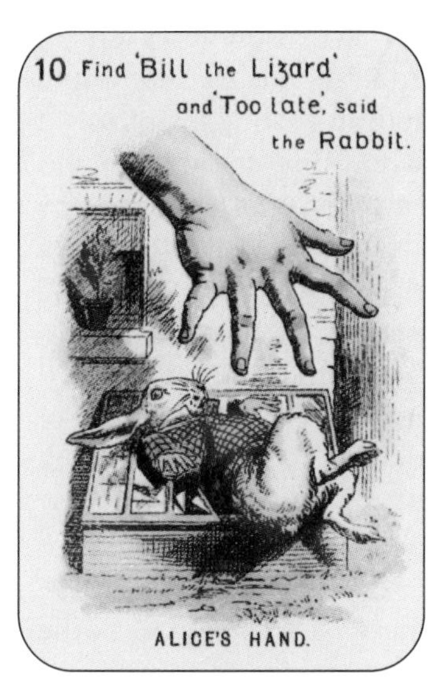

Alice collects nine little cakes. In puzzle number 3 (page 8), Alice made eight rows with three cakes in each row. Using just nine cakes, make nine rows with three cakes in each row. Draw a diagram to show how it is done.

Using the nine little cakes it is also possible to make ten rows with three cakes in each row. Draw a diagram to show how this puzzle is solved.

Alice swallowed one of the cakes and was delighted to find that she began shrinking again.

Puzzle #19 / A Stick I Found

Alice, now very small, ran out of the White Rabbit's house into a wood. She looked up and saw an enormous puppy stretching out one paw, trying to touch her. She picked up a stick, whereupon the puppy jumped into the air with a yelp of delight. Alice used the stick to play with the puppy until it was exhausted.

3

THE PUPPY.

Here is a verse-riddle about a stick:

A stick I found that weighed two pound:
I sawed it up one day
In pieces eight of equal weight!
How much did each piece weigh?

Remember that sixteen ounces make a pound. The answer is not four ounces!

Puzzle #20 / A Mysterious Number

"Who are *you?*" said the Caterpillar. "I hardly know, sir, just at present. think I must have been changed several times," said Alice. "What do you mean by that?" said the Caterpillar sternly. "Explain yourself!"

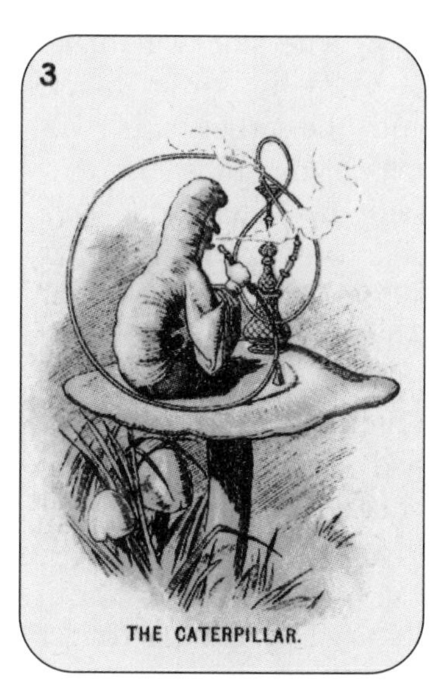

Here is something for you to explain. It concerns a mysterious number that also keeps changing, yet remains the same!

Start with the number **142,857.**

Try multiplying it by **two**, and write down your answer. Now multiply it by **three**. Continue until you get to **six**, recording all your answers. Look closely at the digits in each of your answers.

What do you notice?

Now multiply the mysterious number by **seven**. Can you "explain yourself" and make sense of these answers?

Puzzle #21 / Cryptogram

"One side will make you grow taller, and the other side will make you grow shorter," said the Caterpillar. "One side of *what*? The other side of *what*?" thought Alice to herself. "Of the mushroom," said the Caterpillar, just as if she had asked it aloud; and in another moment it was out of sight.

In a cryptogram, one set of letters is exchanged for another. For example, ALICE SAID might be written as PKTIF QPTZ, where A becomes P, L becomes K, I becomes T, etc. Decode this poem written by Lewis Carroll:

"HXS NET XPO, ANIWTE GCPPCNV," IWT HXSJL VNJ MNCO,
"NJO HXSE WNCE WNM DTRXVT YTEH GWCIT;
NJO HTI HXS CJRTMMNJIPH MINJO XJ HXSE WTNO —
OX HXS IWCJF, NI HXSE NLT, CI CM ECLWI?"

Puzzle #22 / Who's Coming to Dinner?

Alice folded her hands, and began to repeat . .

THE ENQUIRING YOUTH.

"You are old," said the youth, "and your jaws are too weak for anything tougher than suet. Yet you finished the goose, with the bones and the beak. Pray how did you manage to do it?"

It was a strange dinner party at which Father William ate the bones and beak of the goose.

At another dinner party, he invited a small number of people to join him. The guests included his father's brother-in-law, his brother's father-in-law, his father-in-law's brother, and his brother-in-law's father. How many guests were invited if the number attending is to be the absolute minimum?

If the answer is not four guests, explain the result.

Puzzle #23 / Upside Down

Father William was famed for standing on his head. He had another talent. "You are old," said the youth, "one would hardly suppose that your eye was as steady as ever. Yet you balanced an eel on the end of your nose. What made you so awfully clever?"

Here is a triangle of ten little cakes. By moving just three cakes, make the triangle turn upside down.

O

O O

O O O

O O O O

Puzzle #24 / Dreaming

The youth wanted to know what made him so awfully clever.

THE YOUTH ASTOUNDED.

"I have answered three questions, and that is enough," said his father; "don't give yourself airs! Do you think I can listen all day to such stuff? Be off, or I'll kick you down stairs!"

Here is a question in the form of a verse-riddle to tell just how clever you are.

Dreaming of apples on a wall,
And dreaming often, dear,
I dreamed that, if I counted all,
— How many would appear?

How many apples appeared in the dream? The answer is given in the poem.

Puzzle #25 / Consecutive Letters

Alice swallowed a morsel of the mushroom but found that she now had an immense length of neck that seemed to rise like a stalk out of a sea of green leaves that lay far below her. She tried to get her head down, and was delighted to find that her neck would bend about easily in any direction. "Serpent!" screamed the Pigeon.

Take two consecutive letters from each of these characters in Wonderland, and put them together to make a fourth character:

MAGPIE

HEDGEHOG

GRYPHON

Puzzle #26 / Eggs in a Row

"As if it wasn't trouble enough hatching the eggs," said the Pigeon; "but I must be on the look-out for serpents night and day! I suppose you'll be telling me next that you never tasted an egg!" "I *have* tasted eggs, certainly," said Alice, who was a very truthful child.

THE PIGEON'S NEST.

This is another arrangement problem. Imagine that you have ten eggs that are equally spaced in two rows of five, as shown in the diagram:

Move any four eggs to make five rows with exactly four eggs in each row. The other six eggs must remain in the same initial position.

Puzzle #27 / A Serpentile Letter

"I'm *not* a serpent!" said Alice indignantly. "Well! *What* are you?" said the Pigeon. "I can see you're trying to invent something!" "I'm a little girl," said Alice, rather doubtfully. "No, no! You're a serpent, and there's no use denying it."

Here is a serpentile letter that Lewis Carroll sent to a child friend. Can you work out what it says?

Why, how can she know that no harm has come to it? Surely I must know best, having the book before me from morning to night, and gazing at it for hours together with tear-dimmed eyes? Why, there were several things I didn't even mention, for instance, the number of beetles that had got crushed between the leaves. So when I sign myself 'your loving' you go down a step, and say 'your affectionate'?? Very well, then I go down another step, and sign myself! truly, Lewis Carroll. Oct. 22/78

Puzzle #28 / Postal Magic Square

Alice came upon a little house. A footman in livery came running and rapped loudly at the door. The Fish-Footman began by producing from under his arm a great letter, nearly as large as himself, and this he handed over saying, in a solemn tone, "For the Duchess. An invitation from the Queen to play croquet."

Here is a puzzle about postage stamps. In Victorian times, these were the nine smallest stamps in use:

½d, 1d, 1½d, 2d, 2½d, 3d, 3½d, 4d, 5d

By placing the stamps on a 3 x 3 grid, make each row, column, and diagonal total to the same amount. You may use ten stamps; that is, one each of the above amounts and one extra from the list. On one square you may place two stamps.

Puzzle #29 / A Number of Letters

Then the Frog-Footman repeated, in the same solemn tone, only changing the order of the words a little, "From the Queen. An invitation for the Duchess to play croquet." Then they both bowed low, and their curls got entangled together. Alice laughed so much that she had to run back into the wood for fear of their hearing her.

This puzzle may appear, in the first instance, not to be about letters, but about numbers instead. However, look more closely, and you will discover that letters, not necessarily of the postage variety, play their part.

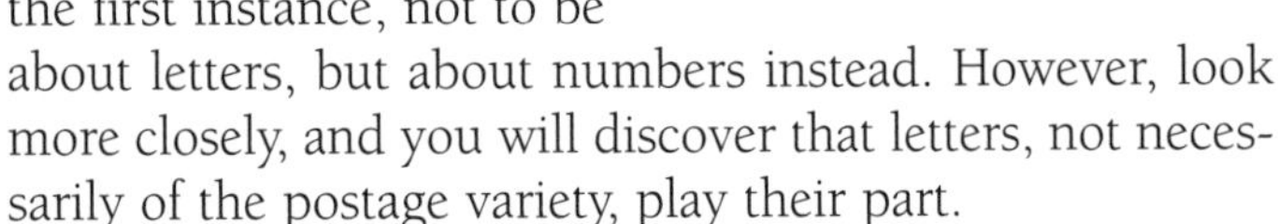

The problem is to take two from eleven and make the result even.

Puzzle #30 / Cipher

THE DUCHESS WITH BABY.

The door led right into a large kitchen. The Duchess was sitting on a three-legged stool, nursing a baby. The cook was stirring a large cauldron of soup. "There's certainly too much pepper in that soup!" said Alice to herself, as well as she could for sneezing. Even the Duchess sneezed occasionally.

Here is an extract from *Alice's Adventures in Wonderland* written in the Telegraph Cipher devised by Lewis Carroll. The instructions to decode the message are given on the following pages.

"Mhncu'b ukovrlliy vra fzwm hkqznc qg dbfv zfee!" eoxl Riqrs vr hncgplj. Mhncu xww dkaayljdh vdf mzuh rj ja qg dhb ojc. Uysb mhn Qerpknw zgupxkc apryboasogia, tjl mhn sysy sfw zgupxgsi rgv misugen. Fms asdt arljin ge arp mgmmkpl apom ljq lfd wsknuu xsxb vkp wfie, fbo t ntfib mra cmomy srb gldvxbl nhljbxbl ohfx kfx yf utf.

This is not a substitution cryptogram. To decode the extract, the keyword "forty-two" is needed.

THE TELEGRAPH CIPHER

(devised by Lewis Carroll in April 1868.)

The instructions for using the cipher are as follows:

KEY ALPHABET

a b c d e f g h i j k l m n o p q r s t u v w x y z

---

a b c d e f g h i j k l m n o p q r s t u v w x y z a

MESSAGE ALPHABET

1. Copy the above onto a card and cut the card in two along the line.

2. In order to send messages in this cipher, a keyword must be agreed between the correspondents: this should be carried in the memory only.

3. To translate a message into cipher, write the keyword, letter for letter, over the message, repeating it as often as may be necessary: slide the message-cipher along under the other, so as to bring the first letter of the message under the first letter of the keyword, and copy the letter that stands over "a": then do the same with the second letter of the message and the second letter of the keyword, and so on.

4. Translate the cipher back into English by the same process.

Example

keyword	t	r	i	c	k	t	r	i	c	k	t	r
message	c	o	m	e	t	o	m	o	r	r	o	w
cipher	r	d	w	y	r	f	f	u	l	t	f	v

To translate back again:

keyword	t	r	i	c	k	t	r	i	c	k	t	r
cipher	r	d	w	y	r	f	f	u	l	t	f	v
message	c	o	m	e	t	o	m	o	r	r	o	w

Puzzle #31 / Fair Shares

The cook took the cauldron of soup off the fire, and set to work throwing everything within her reach at the Duchess and the baby. The fire irons came first, then a shower of saucepans, plates, and dishes. The Duchess took no notice of them even when they hit her.

The generous cook shared the kitchen utensils among the characters in the Duchess' house. This next problem is about sharing out a sum of money fairly between two brothers.

Two brothers are left some money, amounting to an exact number of dollars. It is to be shared fairly between them. The elder undertook the division.

"But your heap is larger than mine!" cried the younger.

"True," said the elder. "Allow me to present you with one-third of my heap."

The Younger added it to his heap, and after looking thoughtfully at the now gigantic pyramid, he suddenly exclaimed "I am well off now! Here is half the heap for you."

"You are generous," said the other, as he swept up the money. "Two-thirds of this heap is the least I can offer you."

"I will not be outdone in generosity!" cried the younger, hastily handing over three-quarters of his property.

"Prudence is a virtue," remarked the elder. "Content yourself with two-thirds of my present wealth."

"One-third of mine is all I can now afford!" retorted the other.

"And now, if I give you one dollar," remarked the elder brother, "we shall, I think, be square?"

He was right. How much money was divided between them?

This problem, invented by Lewis Carroll, has been slightly modified to fit the currency of the United States. There is probably more than one solution to the problem. See if you can find the smallest number of dollars that may be divided between the two brothers following the conditions given in the conversation.

Puzzle #32 / Transformation

The Duchess sang a sort of lullaby to the baby, tossing it violently up and down. The poor thing howled so, that Alice could hardly hear the words. "Here! you may nurse it a bit, if you like!" the Duchess said to Alice, flinging the baby at her as she spoke. "I must go and get ready to play croquet with the Queen."

ALICE AND THE PIG BABY.

The baby grunted, and Alice looked anxiously into its face to see what was the matter with it. It had a very turned-up nose. The baby grunted again. There was no mistake about it: it was neither more nor less than a pig.

Use the same rules for *Doublets*, which are given for puzzle number 9 (page 14), change COOK into BABY, and drive the PIG into a STY.

Puzzle #33 / Cat Food

Alice saw a Cheshire Cat sitting on a bough of a tree. The Cat only grinned when it saw Alice. It looked good-natured, she thought: still it had *very* long claws and a great many teeth, so she felt that it ought to be treated with respect.

ALICE AND THE CHESHIRE CAT.

This puzzle is another verse-riddle. The problem is to explain the conduct of the cat.

Three sisters at breakfast were feeding the cat,
The first gave it sole — Puss was grateful for that:
The next gave it salmon — which Puss thought a treat:
The third gave it herring — which Puss wouldn't eat.

Why did the cat refuse the food offered by the third sister?

Puzzle #34 / Which Clock?

Alice asked the Cheshire Cat, "Which way I ought to go from here?" "That depends a good deal on where you want to get to," said the Cat. "I don't much care where," said Alice. "Then it doesn't matter which way you go," the Cat replied. Then the Cat slowly vanished, beginning with the end of the tail, and ending with the grin, which remained some time after the rest had gone.

It didn't matter which direction Alice chose to take, because she was sure to get somewhere. However, here is a choice, and it makes a great deal of difference which one is selected. There are two clocks. You have the choice of one of them. The first clock is right only once a year, the other is right twice every day. Which one do you choose, and why'?

Puzzle #35 / The Hatter's Riddle

There was a table set out under a tree in front of a house, and the March Hare and the Hatter were having tea at it. "No room! No room!" they cried. "There's *plenty* of room!" said Alice indignantly, and she sat down in a large armchair at one end of the table.

"TWINKLE, TWINKLE," said the HATTER.

The Hatter opened his eyes very wide and said,

"Why is a raven like a writing desk?"

Alice thought that she could guess the answer to this riddle. "Do you mean that you think you can find out the answer to it?" said the March Hare. "Exactly so," said Alice. "Then you should say what you mean," the March Hare went on. A little later the Hatter said, "Have you guessed the riddle yet?" "No, I give it up," replied Alice: "what's the answer?" "I haven't the slightest idea," said the Hatter.

But the Hatter's riddle does have solutions. Can you find one?

Puzzle #36 / A Mad Tea Party

"Wake up, Dormouse!" they both cried. The Dormouse slowly opened his eyes. "Tell us a story!" said the March Hare. "And be quick about it," added the Hatter. The Dormouse told the story, and then fell asleep instantly. Alice left the tea party, and as she looked back she saw them trying to put the Dormouse into the teapot.

THE DORMOUSE IN THE TEAPOT.

In this verse-riddle, the answer is partly connected with a tea party:

A monument, men all agree, am I in all sincerity,
Half cat, half hindrance made.
If head and tail removed should be,
Then most of all you strengthen me:
Replace my head, the stand you see
On which my tail is laid.

Puzzle #37 / Painted Cubes

A large rose tree stood near the entrance of the garden: the roses growing on it were white, but there were three gardeners at it, busily painting them *red*. "Why are you painting those roses?" said Alice. "You see, Miss, this here ought to have been a *red* rose tree, and we put a white one in by mistake," said Two.

GARDENERS TWO AND FIVE.

This problem is about painting. Imagine that you have some wooden cubes. You also have six paint tins each containing a *different* colour of paint. You paint a cube using a *different* colour for each of the six faces. How many *different* cubes can be painted using the same set of six colours?

Remember that two cubes are different only when it is not possible, by turning one, to make it correspond with the other.

Game #38 / An Odd Card

"If the Queen was to find out, we should all have our heads cut off, you know," said Two. At this moment, Five, who had been anxiously looking across the garden, called out "The Queen! The Queen!" and the three gardeners threw themselves flat on their faces.

GARDENER SEVEN.

The three playing-card gardeners were, of course, spades; numbers two, three, and seven. In this next problem, the solution is similar to that for puzzle number 29 (page 34). If you solved that puzzle, then this will be very easy for you.

In this problem, all you have to do is:

take one from seven and make it even.

Game #39 / Court Circular

The procession included soldiers carrying clubs, courtiers ornamented with diamonds, royal children dressed in hearts, and other guests, mostly Kings and Queens. Then followed the Knave of Hearts, carrying the King's crown on a crimson velvet cushion; and, last of all, the King and Queen of Hearts.

The procession, of course, was made up of playing cards. Lewis Carroll invented and published a card game in 1862 calling it *Court Circular.*

First-Hand

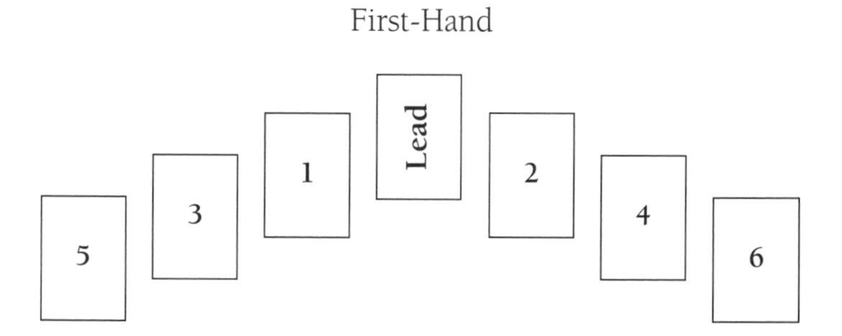

I

Cut for deal; highest is "first-hand," lowest is dealer, and gives six cards to each, three at a time, turning up the thirteenth as "Lead." Firsthand then plays a card, then dealer, and so on, as numbered in the diagram, till six have been played, when the trick is complete. No. 5 is kept face down until No. 6 has been played.

II

Whichever has, on his side of the trick, (Lead reckoning on each side,) the best "Line" of three cards, (Lines being of three kinds, which rank as follows: "Trio," e.g. three Kings or three Nines; "Sequence," e.g. Nine of Hearts, Eight of Spades, Seven of Hearts; "Suit," e.g. three Diamonds) wins it. It does not matter in what order the cards have been played, (e.g. if Lead be Five of Hearts, and one of the players plays Ace of Spades, Seven of Clubs, Six of Diamonds, his side contains a Sequence). Trio containing Lead ranks above Trio not containing it, and so of Sequence and Suit. Lead must not be reckoned as the middle card of a Sequence. An Ace will form a Sequence with Two, Three, or with King, Queen.

III

If equal Lines be made, he who has played, among the cards forming his Line, the best card, (cards ranking thus: Ace of Hearts, of Diamonds, of Clubs, of Spades, King of Hearts, etc.) wins the trick; if no Line be made, he who has played the best card wins it.

IV

When the trick is won by superiority of Line, the winner adds the value of his own Line, (reckoned thus: Trio 1, Sequence 2, Suit 3) to that of the loser's, if any, (reckoned thus: Trio 5, Sequence 3, Suit I,) and takes so many cards; when by superiority of cards, he takes one only. Lead for the next trick is then chosen from the cards left on the table, (by the winner, if both or neither have made a Line; otherwise, by the loser,) and the others laid aside. The loser is dealer for the next trick, and gives three cards to each.

V

When only three cards remain to be dealt, they are turned up, and each plays, either from the three cards in his hand, or from these three, supplying its place from his own hand.

VI

When the pack is out, every trick (after four) counts 1; most cards, 2; most court cards, (Aces reckoning as court cards,) 1. A Hit is 5, and two Hits make a Rubber.

Puzzle #40 / Off With Their Heads!

"And who are *these*?" said the Queen, pointing to the three gardeners who were lying round the rose tree. The Knave carefully turned them over. "Get up!" said the Queen, "what *have* you been doing here?" "May it please your Majesty," said Two, "we were trying . . ." "I see!" said the Queen, "Off with their heads!"

Here are some more *Doublets*. The rules are given on page 14.

Make HEAD into TAIL
OPEN the GATE
CRY OUT
Put the HORSE out to GRASS

Game #41 / Arithmetical Croquet

"Can you play croquet?" shouted the Queen. "Yes!" shouted Alice. "Come on, then!" roared the Queen. Alice thought she had never seen such a curious croquet ground; the balls were live hedgehogs, the mallets live flamingoes, and the soldiers had to double themselves up and to stand upon their hands and feet, to make the arches.

ALICE AND THE FLAMINGO.

Lewis Carroll invented a game for two players called *Arithmetical Croquet*. You can either play it on paper, or later, when you get more accomplished, you can play it just using your head.

RULES

1. The first player names a number not greater than eight: the second does the same: the first then names a higher number, not advancing more than eight beyond his last; and so on alternately. Whoever names 100, which is the "winning peg," wins the game.

2. The numbers 10, 20, etc. are the "hoops." To "take" a hoop, it is necessary to go from a number below it to one the same distance above it: e.g. to go from 17 to 23 would "take" the hoop 20; but to go to any other number above 20 would "miss it," in which case the player in his next turn would have to go back to a number below 20 in order to "take" it properly. To miss a hoop twice loses the game.

3. It is also lawful to "take" a hoop by playing *into* it, in one turn, and out of it to the same distance above it, in the next turn: e.g. to play from 17 to 20, and then from 20 to 23 in the next turn, would "take" the hoop 20. A player "in" a hoop may not play out of it with any other than the number so ordered.

4. Whatever step one player takes, bars the other from taking an equal step, or the difference between it and 9: e.g. if one player advances two, the other may not advance two or seven. But a player has no "barring" power when playing *into* a hoop, or when playing from any number between 90 and 100, unless the other player is also at such a number.

5. The "winning peg," like the "hoops," may be "missed" once, but to miss it twice loses the game.

6. When one player is "in" a hoop, the other can keep him in, by playing the number he needs for coming out, so as to bar him from using it. He can also do it by playing the difference between this and 9. And he

may thus go on playing the two barring numbers alternately: but he may not play either twice running; e.g. if one player has gone from 17 to 20, the other can keep him in by playing 3, 6, 3, 6, etc.

The games takes some practice, but once the rules have been memorised, a great deal of fun can be gained. The game helps to make the players adept at mental arithmetic.

Puzzle #42 / A Tale of More Heads

The Cheshire Cat's head appeared. There was a dispute between the executioner, the King, and the Queen. The executioner's argument was, that you couldn't cut off a head unless there was a body to cut it off from. The King said that anything that had a head could be beheaded. However, the Cat's head just faded away.

Talking of "heads," here is a puzzle about tossing coins. Suppose that a coin is tossed several times, and the condition is that if it lands as a "head" once, then the player gets 1 dollar; if two "heads" in succession, an additional 2 dollars is added to the winnings; if three "heads" in a row, then an additional 4 dollars is won; and so on, doubling for each successful throw.

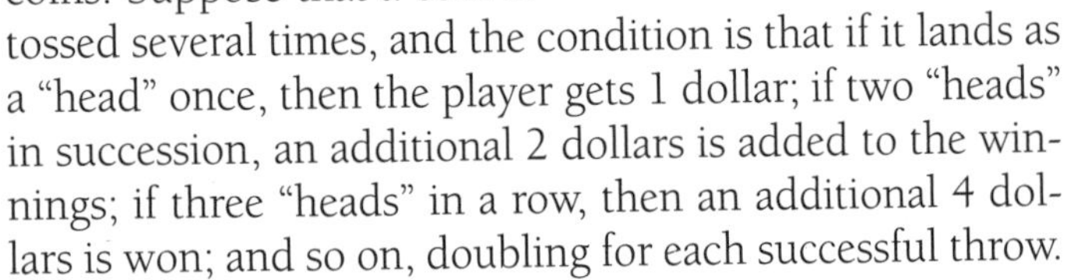

What are the long-term prospects for playing this game?

Puzzle #43 / The King's First Problem

When Alice appeared, she was appealed to by the executioner, the King, and the Queen to settle the argument. The King argued that they should not talk nonsense. The Queen's argument was, that if something wasn't done about it in less than no time, she'd have everybody executed, all round.

THE KING ARGUING.

In time, the King found that the country was very short of money, and that everyone *must* live more economically. He decided to send away most of his wise men. There were some hundreds of them, very fine old men, and magnificently dressed in green velvet gowns with gold buttons: if they *had* a fault, it was that they always contradicted one another when asked for their advice, and they certainly ate and drank enormously. So, on the whole, he was rather glad to get rid of them. But there was an old law, which he did not dare to disobey, which said that there must always be:

"Seven blind of both eyes:
Ten blind of one eye:
Five that see with both eyes:
Nine that see with one eye."

If this be the case, how many wise men could he keep without disobeying the old law?

This problem was devised by Lewis Carroll, and it appeared in *Aunt Judy's Magazine* in December 1870, being one of seven examples that he called "Puzzles from Wonderland." The other puzzles that are included here are numbered 4 (page 9), 19 (page 24), 27 (page 29), and 33 (page 40).

Puzzle #44 / The Rule of Three

"I quite agree with you," said the Duchess, "and the moral of that is — 'Be what you would seem to be' — or if you'd like it put more simply — 'Never imagine yourself not to be otherwise than what it appears to others that what you were or might have been was not otherwise than what you had been would have appeared to them to be otherwise.' "

THE DUCHESS SMILING.

The rule of three in arithmetic often makes people feel the same way as when you hear the Duchess' moral: very confused! Here is an example of the rule of three taken from the book that Lewis Carroll used when he was at school:

If eight men can do a piece of work in twelve days; in how many days can sixteen men perform the same?

Clearly, it will take sixteen men less time to undertake the same work as eight men; in fact, half the time. Therefore, the solution is six days.

A rule of three problem that Lewis Carroll often posed was the following:

> **If it takes four men one day to build a wall, how long does it take 60,000 men to build a similar wall?**

Another rule of three problem that he gave was:

> **If a cat can kill a rat in a minute, how long would it be killing 60,000 rats?**

The answers are not quite as mathematical as they seem, but are based upon reasonable logic.

Puzzle #45 / A Lesson in Squaring

"We went to school in the sea. The master was an old Turtle. We used to call him Tortoise," said the Mock Turtle. "Why did you call him Tortoise, if he wasn't one?" Alice asked. "We called him Tortoise because he taught us," said the Mock Turtle. "You ought to be ashamed of yourself for asking such a simple question," added the Gryphon.

THE GRYPHON.

Lewis Carroll was good in arithmetic at school. Later in life he devised many mathematical questions. Here is one of his problems about square numbers:

Prove that three times the sum of three square numbers is also the sum of four squares. As a starter, you might like to show that double the sum of two square numbers can be written as the sum of two squares.

Puzzle #46 / A Lesson in Uglification

"I only took the regular course." "What was that?" inquired Alice. "Reeling and Writhing to begin with," the Mock Turtle replied, "and then the different branches of Arithmetic — Ambition, Distraction, Uglification, and Derision."

In Lewis Carroll's nonsense poem, *The Hunting of the Snark*, the fifth stanza contains some arithmetic. What is the answer?

Taking Three as the subject to reason about —
A convenient number to state —
We add Seven, and Ten, and then multiply out
By One Thousand diminished by Eight.

The result we proceed to divide, as you see,
By Nine Hundred and Ninety and Two:
Then subtract Seventeen, and the answer must be
Exactly and perfectly true.

Try with other numbers. Why do you get these results?

Puzzle #47 / Character Wordsearch (2)

'Tis the voice of the Lobster; I heard him declare. You have baked me too brown, I must sugar my hair. As a duck with its eyelids, so he with his nose, trims his belt and his buttons, and turns out his toes.

In this wordsearch, apart from the Lobster, there are eight other creatures from Wonderland for you to find:

L	O	B	S	T	E	R	R	N	F
E	X	Y	W	O	A	E	T	W	I
S	P	M	I	R	H	S	H	A	N
I	H	A	T	T	S	I	T	Y	O
O	P	D	N	O	T	O	U	W	H
P	R	A	Q	I	E	Z	R	A	P
R	P	K	N	S	L	E	T	B	Y
O	S	G	I	E	U	M	L	M	R
P	X	A	Q	U	F	I	E	N	G

Puzzle #48 / Diagonal Acrostic

"The trial's beginning!" The King and Queen of Hearts were seated on their throne, and near the King was the White Rabbit, with trumpet in hand, and a scroll of parchment in the other. "Herald, read the accusation!" said the King.

In this puzzle, arrange the names of these six characters from Wonderland into this 6 x 6 grid so that reading along the left to right diagonal, the name of another character appears.

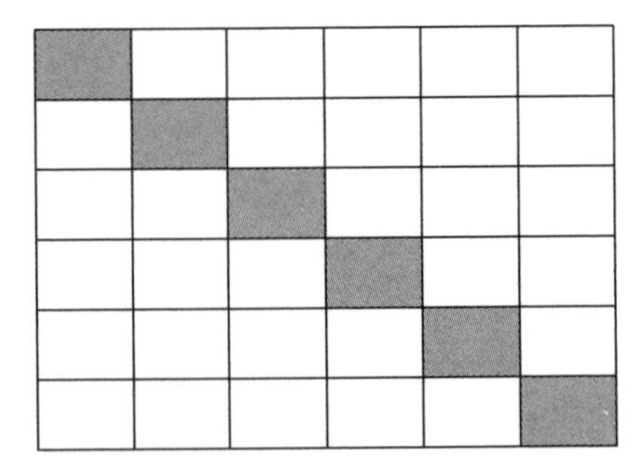

TURTLE
RABBIT
MORCAR
FATHER
FERRET
HERALD

Puzzle #49 / The King's Second Problem

"Consider your verdict," the King said to the jury. "Not yet, not yet!" the Rabbit hastily interrupted. "There's a great deal to come before that!" "Call the first witness," said the King; and the White Rabbit blew three blasts on the trumpet.

THE KING IN COURT.

In the palace, the King had a favourite room with only one window in it, a square window, 3 feet high and 3 feet wide. Now he had weak eyes and the window gave too much light, so he sent for the builder and told him to alter it, so as to give half the light. Only, he was to keep it square, he was to keep it 3 feet high, and he was to keep it 3 feet wide. How did he do it? Remember, he wasn't allowed to use curtains, or shutters, or coloured glass, or anything of that sort.

Puzzle #50 / The Queen's Problem

The first witness was the Hatter. "Take off your hat," the King said. "It isn't mine," said the Hatter, "I keep them to sell." Here the Queen put on her spectacles, and began staring hard at the Hatter, who turned pale and fidgeted.

THE QUEEN IN COURT.

A captive Queen and her son and daughter were shut up in the top room of a very high tower. Outside their window was a pulley with a rope round it, and a basket fastened at each end of the rope of equal weight. They managed to escape quite safely with the help of this and a weight they found in the room. It would have been dangerous for any of them to come down if they weighed 15 lbs. more than the contents of the lower basket, for they would do so too quickly, and they also managed not to weigh less either. The one basket coming down would naturally draw the other up. The Queen weighed 195 lbs., her daughter 165 lbs., her son 90 lbs., and the weight 75 lbs. How did they do it?

Game #51 / Lanrick

"You may sit down," the King said. "I'd rather finish my tea," said the Hatter, with an anxious look at the Queen. "You may go," said the King; and the Hatter hurriedly left the court, without even waiting to put his shoes on.

THE HATTER LEAVING THE COURT.

Another game invented by Lewis Carroll, called *Lanrick*, is played on a chessboard. The game is for two players; each player having five men (pawns); the other requisites are a die and shaker, and something (such as a coin) to mark a square. The interior of the board, excluding the border squares, is regarded as containing six rows and six columns. It must be agreed which is the first row and first column.

1. The Players set their men in turn, alternately, on any border squares they like.

2. The die is thrown twice, and a square marked accordingly, the first throw fixing the row, the second, the column; the marked square, with the eight surrounding squares, forms the first "rendezvous," into which the men are to be played.

3. The men move like chess queens; in playing for the first "rendezvous," each Player may move over six squares, either with one man, or dividing the move among several.

4. When one Player has got all his men into the "rendezvous," the other must remove from the board one of his men that has failed to get in; the die is then thrown for a new "rendezvous," for which each Player may move over as many squares as he had men in the last "rendezvous," and one more.

5. If it be found that either Player has all his men already in the new "rendezvous," the die must be thrown again, till a "rendezvous" is found where this is not the case.

6. The Game ends when one Player has lost all his men.

Puzzle #52 / A Russian's Sons

"I *gave her one, they gave him two*, why, that must be what he did with the tarts," said the King. "But it goes on *they all returned from him to you*," said Alice. "Why, there they are!" said the King triumphantly, pointing to the tarts on the table.

Lewis Carroll invented a new kind of riddle in 1892. The novelty is in the method of solution. This example concerns a Russian family.

A Russian had three sons.
The first, named Rab, became a lawyer.
The second, Ymra, became a soldier.
The third became a sailor.
What was his name?

Puzzle #53 / Making Words

"Let the jury consider their verdict," the King said, for about the twentieth time. "No, no!" said the Queen. "Sentence first, verdict afterwards." "Stuff and nonsense!" said Alice loudly. "The idea of having the sentence first!"

The Knave was accused of stealing the tarts:

> The Queen of Hearts, she made some tarts,
> All on a summer day:
> The Knave of Hearts, he stole those tarts,
> And took them quite away!

But the tarts were on a table in the courtroom, which probably makes him not guilty.

See how many different words you can make using the letters in "THE KNAVE." You should be able to find at least twenty-five words without repeating any of the letters (apart from the letter "e," which appears twice).

Puzzle #54 / Alice in Wonderland Acrostic

"Hold your tongue!" said the Queen, turning purple. "I won't!" said Alice. "Off with her head!" the Queen shouted at the top of her voice. Nobody moved. "Who cares for you?" said Alice, "You're nothing but a pack of cards!"

At the end of the second Alice-book, *Through the Looking-Glass*, Lewis Carroll included a poem that reminds us that the story of Alice was written for three little sisters during a boat trip in July 1862. The children eagerly listened to the story of Alice as she went down the rabbit hole and into Wonderland. At the end of the trip, one of the sisters asked Lewis Carroll to write out the story for her so that she would not forget the delights that he had invented for them during that wonderful day. Within the poem is hidden the name of that child, the original Alice in Wonderland. The poem is reproduced on the following page. Can you find her real name?

A Boat, beneath a sunny sky
Lingering onward dreamily
In an evening of July —

Children three that nestle near,
Eager eye and willing ear,
Pleased a simple tale to hear —

Long has paled that sunny sky:
Echoes fade and memories die:
Autumn frosts have slain July.

Still she haunts me, phantomwise.
Alice moving under skies
Never seen by waking eyes.

Children yet, the tale to hear,
Eager eye and willing ear,
Lovingly shall nestle near.

In a Wonderland they lie,
Dreaming as the days go by,
Dreaming as the summers die:

Ever drifting down the stream —
Lingering in a golden gleam —
Life, what is it but a dream?

Solutions

1. The Rabbit Hole:

DISH, WISH, DIP, WASH, WASP, WAFER, WATER, WATCH.

2. The Lovely Garden:

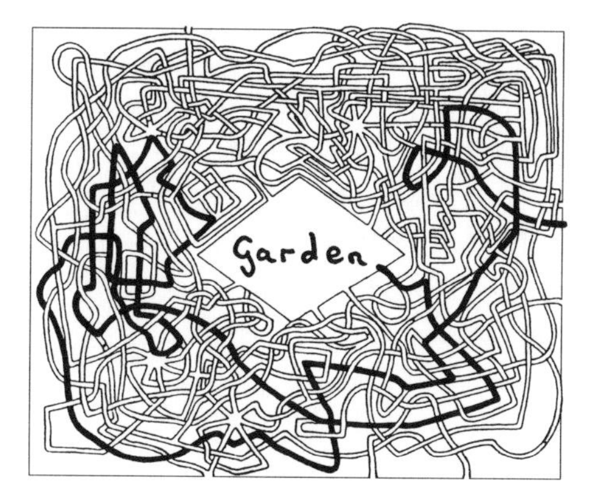

3. Little Cakes (1):

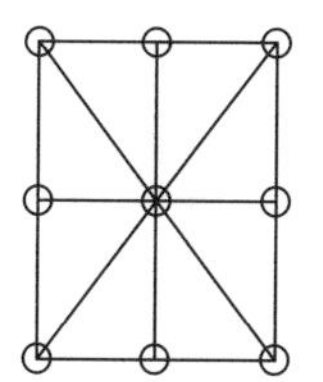

three horizontal rows

three vertical rows

two diagonal rows

4. Two Brothers and a Box:

The "box" was a "box around the ears"!

5. **Who in the World Am I?:**

ADA

6. **How Puzzling It All Is!:**

Normally, multiplication tables go up to twelve times. In this case, Alice would only get to 19.

An alternative answer is that the products are correct, but in different number bases (starting with 18, and going up in 3's). If you continue the pattern, an answer of 20 is not possible.

7. **Who Goes Where?:**

The Queen is in the Garden.
The Duchess is in the Kitchen.
The Hatter is at the Trial.
The Dormouse is in the Teapot.
The Caterpillar is on the Mushroom.

8. **Character Crossword (1):**

R	A	V	E	N
■	L	■	V	■
D	I	N	A	H
■	C	■	D	■
S	E	V	E	N

9. **Doublets:**

CAT - COT - DOT (or COG) - DOG

FOUR - FOUL - FOOL - FOOT - FORT -
FORE - FIRE - FIVE

10. **Three Squares:**

Hint: Either work from the inside towards the outer edges, or from the outside to the inner edges.

11. **Word Jumble:**

EAGLET, DUCK, DODO, CRAB, MOUSE, BIRD, MAGPIE, and CANARY

12. **Character Crossword (2):**

EAGLET and HATTER

13. **Who's Telling the Truth?:**

The Lory is telling the truth.

15. **Thimbles:**

Since the tumblers were originally filled to the same level, they will again be equally full after the transactions of exchanging thimblefuls of brandy and then the mixture. The volume of brandy now missing from the first tumbler has been replaced by water from the second tumbler. Similarly, the amount of water missing from the second tumbler has been replaced by brandy from the first tumbler. The amount of brandy or water transferred is exactly the same in each case.

16. Character Wordsearch (1):

These characters are hidden in the wordsearch:

Eaglet, Duck, Magpie,
Canary, Bird, Mouse,
Crab, and Lory.

17. On the Roof!:

TILES - TILLS - TELLS - SELLS - SEALS - SEARS - STARS - STARE - STATE - SLATE

KICK - LICK - LACK - LACE - LANE - LAND

BOOTED - BOOKED - ROOKED - ROCKED - ROCKET

18. Little Cakes (2):

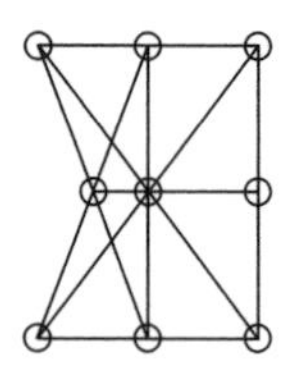

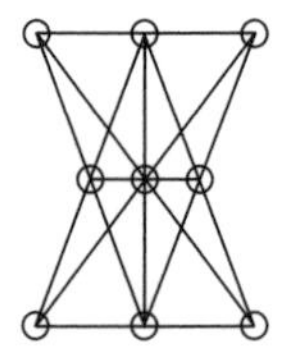

19. A Stick I Found:

When the stick is sawn into pieces, some sawdust is lost; hence the eight pieces weigh a little less than four ounces each.

20. A Mysterious Number:

The number 142,857 is the first six decimal places of one–seventh. These numbers recur.

142,857 x 2 gives 285,714
x 3 gives 428,571
x 4 gives 571,428
x 5 gives 714,285
x 6 gives 857,142

The same digits appear in each answer, keeping the same order but circulating.

142,857 x 7 gives 999,999.

This result is linked to the answer you get when multiplying one-seventh by seven; the answer should be 1 or 0.999999, but the error in the latter result is caused by limiting the original number to only six decimal places.

21. Cryptogram:

"You are old, Father William," the young man said,
"And your hair has become very white;
And yet you incessantly stand on your head —
Do you think, at your age, it is right?"

22. Who's Coming to Dinner?:

There is only one guest. In this family tree, males are shown by uppercase letters, and females by lowercase letters. The host is E and his guest is C.

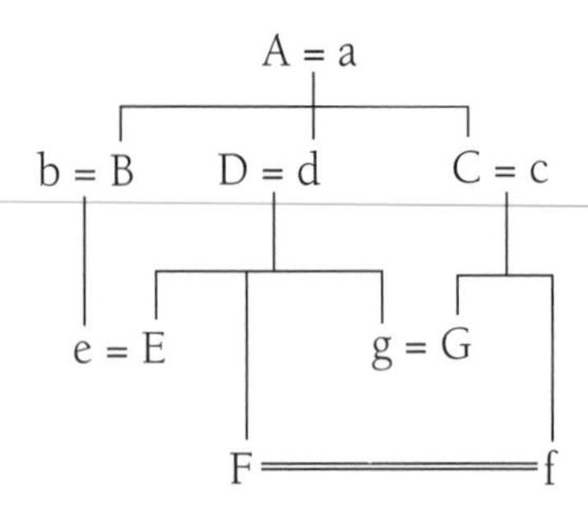

23. Upside Down:

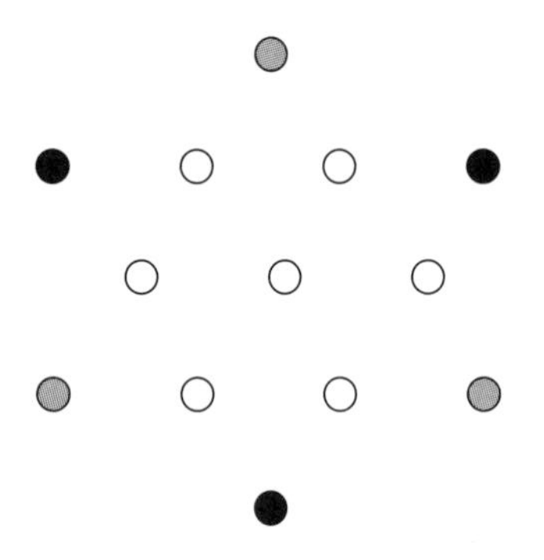

Move the shaded dots to the positions shown by the black dots.

24. Dreaming:

The answer is ten apples.

This comes from the second line of the verse:
"And dreaming of-ten, dear."

25. Consecutive Letters:

Take "PI" from Magpie,
"GE" from Hedgehog,
and "ON" from Gryphon.

Put them together to make PIGEON.

26. Eggs in a Row:

One possible solution is:

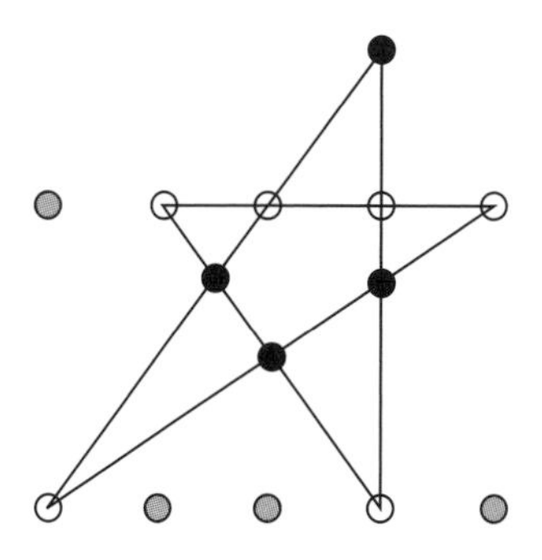

The shaded dots have moved to the position of the white dots, and the black dots have remained in the same place.

27. A Serpentile Letter:

"Why, how can she know that no harm has come to it? Surely I must know best, having the book before me from morning to night, and gazing at it for hours together with tear-dimmed eyes? Why, there were several things I didn't even mention, for instance, the number of beetles that had got crushed between the leaves. So when I sign myself "your loving" you go down a step, and say "your affectionate"? Very well, then I go down another step, and sign myself "yours truly, Lewis Carroll." October 22, 1878.

28. Postal Magic Square:

The 4d stamp is used twice. On one square, the ½d stamp and one of the 4d stamps are placed. The Postal Magic Square when completed looks like this:

2½d	5d	1½d
2d	3d	4d
4½d	1d	3½d

29. A Number of Letters:

The result is achieved as follows:

~~EL~~EVEN

30. Cipher:

The extract when deciphered reads:

"There's certainly too much pepper in that soup!" said Alice to herself. There was certainly too much of it in the air. Even the Duchess sneezed occasionally, and the baby was sneezing and howling. The only things in the kitchen that did not sneeze were the cook, and a large cat which was sitting grinning from ear to ear.

31. Fair Shares:

One possible answer is $80, which was divided up between them in the following stages:

Elder	Younger
$42	$38
$28	$52
$54	$26
$18	$62
$64.50	$15.50
$21.50	$58.50
$41	$39
$40	$40

32. Transformation:

COOK - HOOK - HOOD - GOOD - GOLD - BOLD - BALD - BALE - BABE - BABY

PIG - WIG - WAG - SAG - SAY - STY

33. Cat Food:

That salmon and sole Puss should think very grand
Is no such remarkable thing
For more of these dainties Puss took up her stand;
But when the third sister stretched out her fair hand
Pray why should Puss swallow her ring?

"Herring" was in fact "her ring."

34. Which Clock?:

The clock that is right only once a year (probably losing or gaining a little every day) is the better one; the other is broken and the hands do not move.

35. The Hatter's Riddle:

Lewis Carroll gave his own solution many years after the riddle had been posed:

I may as well put on record here what seems to me to be a fairly appropriate answer, viz. "Because it can produce a few notes, though they are very flat; and it is nevar put with the wrong end in front!" This, however, is merely an afterthought: the Riddle, as originally invented, had no answer at all.

Notice the way he spelt "never" which reverses to give "raven." Other solutions to the riddle which have been suggested are:

Because Poe wrote on both.
Because it slopes with a flap.
Because there is a "b" in both.
Because both have quills dipped in ink.

36. A Mad Tea Party:

Tablet

37. Painted Cubes:

Thirty different cubes

38. An Odd Card:

~~S~~EVEN

40. Off With Their Heads!:

HEAD - HEAL - TEAL - TELL - TALL - TAIL

OPEN - OVEN - EVEN - EVES - EYES - DYES - DOES - DOTS - DOTE - DATE - GATE

CRY - COY - COT - CUT - OUT

HORSE - HOUSE - ROUSE - ROUTE - ROUTS - BOUTS - BOATS - BRATS - BRASS - GRASS

42. A Tale of More Heads:

The probability of getting a head is 1 in 2, giving the thrower 1 dollar. On average, the thrower will get 1 dollar for half the number of throws; i.e. a half-dollar each throw.

The probability of getting two heads in a row is 1 in 4; the probability of getting three heads in a row is 1 in 8; and so on. Overall, the thrower still gets a return of a half-dollar for every throw, irrespective of the outcome. Hence, after 100 throws, the thrower would expect to have $50. After an infinite number of throws, the thrower would expect to have an infinite number of half-dollars; i.e. a very large sum of money!

43. The King's First Problem:

Sixteen wise men remain without disobeying the old law.

44. The Rule of Three:

Mathematically, assuming that the men work without stopping, the wall is built in 5.76 seconds, but, of course, this is nonsense. Clearly, most of the men would not be able to get anywhere near the wall. The building area would be too overcrowded for any serious construction to take place.

In the case of the cat, it is more likely that the rats would seize the advantage of their numbers and kill the cat!

45. A Lesson in Squaring:

$$2(a^2 + b^2) = (a - b)^2 + (a + b)^2$$

$$3(a^2 + b^2 + c^2) = (a + b + c)^2 + (b - c)^2 + (c - a)^2 + (a - b)^2$$

46. A Lesson in Uglification:

You come back to three, or whatever number you start with. The operations are reversed in the second verse.

47. Character Wordsearch (2):

The Lobster together with these characters:
Gryphon, Tortoise, Panther, Whiting, Shrimp, Turtle, Porpoise, and Eel.

48. Diagonal Acrostic:

H	E	R	A	L	D
R	**A**	B	B	I	T
F	A	**T**	H	E	R
T	U	R	**T**	L	E
F	E	R	R	**E**	T
M	O	R	C	A	**R**

The leading diagonal reveals the HATTER.

49. The King's Second Problem:

The window is altered as follows:

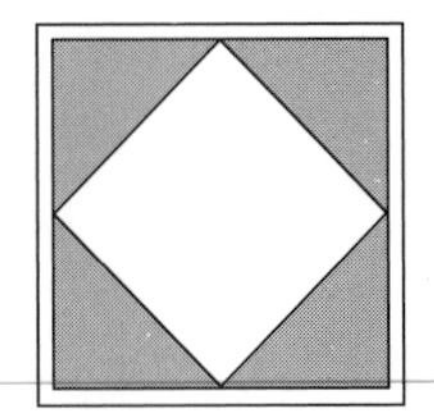

50. The Queen's Problem:

The following table indicates the order in which the Queen and her children make their way to the ground. On some occasions, the weight in both baskets are equal, and it may be assumed that by pulling on the ropes, it is possible to make the appropriate basket reach the ground.

Key: Q, Queen; D, Daughter; S, Son; and W, Weight.

Window level:	QDSW	QDS	QD W	QD
Ground level:		W	S	SW

Q SW	Q S	Q W	DS	D W
D	D W	DS	Q W	Q S

D	SW	S	W
Q SW	QD	QD W	QDS

52. A Russian's Sons:

Yvan (reverse of Navy)

53. Making Words:

Some of the possible words that can be made using the letters in "The Knave" are:

Tea, Tee, Eat, Ate, Eke, Eve, Nee, Van, Tan, Hat, Nave, Neat, Heat, Keen, Knee, Thee, Teak, Vane, Have, Hate, Take, Teen, Even, Heave, Eaten, Haven, Taken, Heaven.

54. Alice in Wonderland Acrostic:

The first letter of each line spells out

ALICE PLEASANCE LIDDEL

the daughter of Dean Liddell, and Lewis Carroll's inspiration to write the story. Alice Liddell was ten years old when Lewis Carroll first told the story to amuse her and her two sisters, Lorina and Edith, during a boat trip on 4 July, 1862, up the River Isis at Oxford. The story was written out in manuscript by Lewis Carroll and given to Alice Liddell as a Christmas present in 1864. The book was published the following year, and has never been out of print.

If you would like to know more about Lewis Carroll and Alice, then write to:

The Lewis Carroll Society of North America,
Mrs. Maxine Schaefer, Secretary,
617 Rockford Road,
Silver Spring,
MD 20902, U.S.A.

or

The Lewis Carroll Society,
Mrs Sarah Stanfield, Secretary,
Little Folly, 105 The Street,
Willesborough,
Ashford, Kent,
TN24 0NB, England.

*****